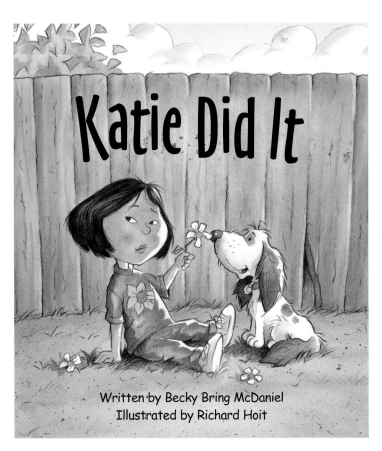

Katie Did It

Written by Becky Bring McDaniel
Illustrated by Richard Hoit

Children's Press®
A Division of Scholastic Inc.
New York • Toronto • London • Auckland • Sydney
Mexico City • New Delhi • Hong Kong
Danbury, Connecticut

Dedicated with all my love to my husband, Larry,
and our three children.—B.B.M

Roger and Fran Gee, in appreciation of your support and
encouragement, this book is dedicated to you both.—R.H.

Reading Consultants

Linda Cornwell
Literacy Specialist

Katharine A. Kane
Education Consultant
(Retired, San Diego County Office of Education
and San Diego State University)

Library of Congress Cataloging-in-Publication Data

McDaniel, Becky Bring.
  Katie did it / written by Becky Bring McDaniel ; illustrated by Richard Hoit.
      p. cm. — (Rookie reader)
  Summary: Katie is a youngest child whose brother and sister seem to blame her for
  everything, but sometimes it's good to know that "Katie did it."
  ISBN 0-516-22848-X (lib. bdg.)   0-516-27832-0 (pbk.)
  [1. Brothers and sisters—Fiction.] I. Hoit, Richard, ill. II. Title. III. Series.
  PZ7.M478417 Kat 2003
  [E]—dc21

                        2002008797

CHILDREN'S PRESS, AND A ROOKIE READER®, and associated logos are
trademarks and or registered trademarks of Grolier Publishing Co., Inc.
SCHOLASTIC and associated logos are trademarks and or registered trademarks
of Scholastic Inc.
1 2 3 4 5 6 7 8 9 10 R 12 11 10 09 08 07 06 05 04 03

Katie was little.

Her brother Kris was bigger.

And her sister Jenny
was even bigger.

Whenever milk was spilled,

Kris and Jenny said, "Katie did it!"

Whenever a ball was left out,

Kris and Jenny said, "Katie did it!"

When the light was left on,

Jenny and Kris said, "Katie did it!"

When the door was left open,

Jenny and Kris said, "Katie did it!"

"Katie did it! Katie did it!"
That was all Katie heard.

25

That day, Mommy called Jenny,
Kris, and Katie inside.

She asked, "Who gave me the pretty flowers?"

And do you know what Katie did?

Katie said, "Katie did it!"

Word List (45 words)

a	did	it	milk	spilled
all	do	Jenny	Mommy	that
and	door	Katie	on	the
asked	even	know	open	was
ball	flowers	Kris	out	what
bigger	gave	left	pretty	when
brother	heard	light	said	whenever
called	her	little	she	who
day	inside	me	sister	you

About the Author

Becky Bring McDaniel was born in Ashland, Ohio, but spent about half of her life in Gainesville, Florida, where she earned her degree in creative writing at the University of Florida. Several of her poems have been published in magazines, and she has written numerous children's books. She is married and has three children.

About the Illustrator

Richard Hoit is a New Zealand-based freelance illustrator. Studying art and art history, Richard has had a passion for drawing and painting all his life. From posters to blankets to cookie tins, Richard now works full-time on children's book illustrations. His work appears in books worldwide.